Adventures From Wales

Edited By Jenni Harrison

First published in Great Britain in 2018 by:

 Young**Writers**

Young Writers
Remus House
Coltsfoot Drive
Peterborough
PE2 9BF
Telephone: 01733 890066
Website: www.youngwriters.co.uk

FOREWORD

Young Writers was created in 1991 with the express purpose of promoting and encouraging creative writing. Each competition we create is tailored to the relevant age group, hopefully giving each child the inspiration and incentive to create their own piece of work, whether it's a poem or a short story. We truly believe that seeing their work in print gives pupils a sense of achievement and pride in their work and themselves.

Every day children bring their toys to life, creating fantastic worlds and exciting adventures, using nothing more than the power of their imagination. What better subject then for primary school pupils to write about, capturing these ideas in a mini saga – a story of just 100 words. With so few words to work with, these young writers have really had to consider their words carefully, honing their writing skills so that every word counts towards creating a complete story.

Within these pages you will find stories about toys coming to life when we're not looking and tales of peril when toys go missing or get lost! Some young writers went even further into the idea of play and imagination, and you may find magical lands or fantastic adventures as they explore their creativity. Each one showcases the talent of these budding new writers as they learn the skills of writing, and we hope you are as entertained by them as we are.

CONTENTS

Independent Entries

Stevie Melkevik (8)   1

Creigiau Primary School, Creigiau

James Hughes (9)   2
Jacob Roszkowski (10)   3
Alissa Hastings (10)   4
Sam Swales (10)   5
Taliesin Campbell (10)   6
Cerys Roberts (9)   7
Freya Wetherall (10)   8
Josh Barton (10)   9
Leo Rees (10)   10
Coco Williams (9)   11
Lucia Andrews (9)   12
Lauren Smith (9)   13
Tom Blake (10)   14
Kaitlyn Mair Halsall (10)   15
Courtney Topping-Morris (10)   16
Charlie Cartwright (10)   17
Emily Blake (10)   18
Will Lewis (10)   19
Ellie Prosser (9)   20
Max Jones (9)   21
Sam Scott (10)   22

Hafren Junior School, Newtown

Verity Després-Davies (9)   23
Jessie Roberts (9)   24
Grace Cia Evans (9)   25

Halfway Primary School, Llanelli

Daisy Thomas (10)   26
Lara Louise Staples (10)   27
Julia Murawska (9)   28
Bella Gilbert (10)   29
Nancy Hayes (10)   30
Mason Stickland (9)   31
Sophie Penhaligan (10)   32
Caris Smith (9)   33
Zuzia Kajszcarek (10)   34
Brooke Bell (10)   35
Maddison Ann Morris (9)   36

Hook CP School, Hook

Eva Rose Darlington Douglas (9)   37

Llansawel Primary School, Briton Ferry

Kenneth Evans (9)   38
Chloe Lucia Rees (10) & Jessica   39
Ieuan Evans (11)   40
Kimberley Fowler (11)   41

Llantarnam Community Primary School, Cwmbran

Ejiroghene Divine Adu (10)   42
Alan Yang (9)   43
Rachael Rich (10)   44
Siân Fowler (10)   45
Thomas Clark (9)   46
Connah White (10)   47
Elizabeth Louise Jacobs (10)   48
Jyoti Rai (9)   49

Evie Bloomer (9)   50

Penarlag Primary School, Ewloe

Lorna Jacobs (10)   51
Lucy Elizabeth Davies (8)   52
Lily Burnett (9)   53
Lillia Grace James (10)   54
Molly Catherine Dathan (9)   55
Phoebe Wright (10)   56
Faye Allonby (9)   57

Sandycroft Primary School, Mancot

Alfie George Griffiths (9)   58
Lilly Gibson-Taylor (9)   59
Kacey Summer Nelson (7)   60
Aimee Butler (8)   61
Scarlett Joanna Davies (8)   62
Silvi Ivanova (10)   63
Isabelle Megan Webber (10)   64
Sasha Jackson (8)   65
Lewis Bult (11)   66
Chloe Turner (11)   67
Ossian Rhys Jones (11)   68
Oliver Gilburt (8)   69
Hannah (7)   70
Harrison Finley Webber (8)   71
Imogen Hoyle (10)   72
Carys Williams (8)   73
Paris Finney (10)   74
Nel Boryc (8)   75
Pema Hodgson (9)   76
Alicia Smith (7)   77
Lauren Roberts (10)   78
Tashi Hodgson (7)   79
Lizzy Mills (10)   80
Afon Fewster-Jones (11)   81
Ellie Evans (11)   82
Macy Jones (8)   83
Jayden Bentham Ryan (10)   84
Jade Jenna Wemyss (11)   85
Cameron Gallagher (8)   86

Jessica Bleasdale (11)   87
Tegan-Lily Ellis-Smith (10)   88
Imogen Bell (10)   89
Karina Kasperek (11)   90
Joseph Parry (8)   91
Rhieyen Emily Anne Jones (11)   92
Abigail Paterson (8)   93
Ella Ford (10)   94
Mia Jasmontaite (8)   95
Caitlyn Jones (8)   96
Sara Soghier (8)   97

St Joseph's Primary School, Gabalfa

Evelina Lawrence (7)   98
Ruby Morgan Spain (8)   99
Nandana Suresh (7)   100
Jamie Dafydd Nott (7)   101

Ummul Mumineen Academy, Grangetown

Hana Dualeh (8)   102
Humayra Arish (9)   103

Waunarlwydd Primary School, Waunarlwydd

Jessica Jenkins (11)   104
Kian Lehane (10)   105
Ella Harris (9)   106
Bailey Lewis (10)   107
Matthew James (11)   108
Emily Evans (9)   109
Ruby Oliver (11)   110
Hattie Hughes (10)   111
Tyler Penherwood (11)   112
Lewis William Rees (9)   113
Lily Marie Thomas (10)   114
Daisy Mansell (11)   115
Lewis Hopkins (11)   116
Iyamah Nandra (10)   117
Natasha Cooper (10)   118

Jazmin Rees (9)	119
Saffron Ava Williams (9)	120
Jaydan Paul Davies (11)	121
Ryan Aubrey-Cooze (10)	122
Callum Jeffreys (10)	123
Seren Kathleen Baker (9)	124
Nicole Ashlyn Mort (11)	125
Grace Cope (11)	126
Billy Matthews (10)	127
Evan Williams (11)	128
Josh Stockton (11)	129
Sophie Samamh (11)	130
Lowri Burns (9)	131
Charlie Morgan Davies (10)	132
Caerwyn Richards (11)	133
Callum Stockton (11)	134
Lola Pascoe (10)	135
Sophie Walters (11)	136
Theo Chapman (11)	137
Keira Davies (10)	138
Archie Davies (10)	139
Molly Rees (10)	140
Liam Price (9)	141
Cole Cheetham (10)	142
Kady Marie Davies (9)	143
Mia Cheetham (10)	144
Harley Sinclair (9)	145
Jac Hawkins (11)	146
Mia-Anne Tabone (10)	147

Ysgol Yr Eirl, Trefor

Aron Copeland (10)	148

THE MINI SAGAS

The Magic Football

Once upon a time there lived two brothers, kind Jack and mean Charlie. Jack went outside to play with a football. He kicked it and threw it gently. Then Charlie came outside, and he kicked it very hard, and ripped it. However Charlie did not know that this was a magic football! So when it was the day of the big football tournament the football remembered who had been good and who had been bad. Every shot Charlie took was rubbish, but Jack scored every time and won the trophy for best striker.

Stevie Melkevik (8)

Mission Impossible

"Sergeant," whispered the soldier, "the enemy is asleep."

"Good, let's go."

"Charles, make sure all of the toys are asleep." All the soldiers stood in the centre of the room. "Keep going."

"Matt, scout behind the TV."

"Yes, Sergeant."

"Tom, get the blocks, we're escaping."

"Yes, Sir." As all the soldiers started building a staircase to the door handle, footsteps were heard. "Get back to the box." They all hid or went back to the box. Before the boy went back to sleep, he knocked down the staircase. That is the story of the toy soldiers.

James Hughes (9)
Creigiau Primary School, Creigiau

The Missing Peanut Butter

Banana the cuddly monkey looked in the fridge for some peanut butter, but it was missing. Banana looked everywhere, but he couldn't find it! He told his friend Oink, the silly pig. She said, "Maybe we ran out."
Banana shouted back, "If you're not going to help, I'll carry on looking myself." Banana carried on looking but he still couldn't find it so he screamed, "Arghh." Oink heard so she decided she would help Banana. Both of them looked everywhere but they couldn't find it. They both panicked! Banana whispered, "Did you hear that? Robot's eating the peanut butter. Stop!"

Jacob Roszkowski (10)
Creigiau Primary School, Creigiau

I Am Going To Drop

The naughty alien put the soft, cuddly teddy up on the white, soft toilet roll. "Help!" the teddy shouted. The brave army came running in.
"We will help!"
"I am going to drop!"
Just then, the pink unicorn came, the robot came and the pig full of money came!
"Shut the lid," shouted the army leader.
Unfortunately they didn't shut the lid in time and the teddy dropped in. "Oh no!" Just then, they heard footsteps! It was the little boy. "Hide." So they hid.
"What is Giggle doing in the toilet?" Then the boy got him out.

Alissa Hastings (10)
Creigiau Primary School, Creigiau

The Battle Of The Dinosaur!

It's midnight and the human was asleep. The soldiers came out of the toy box. They were ready for battle against the dinosaurs. "The coast is clear." They came out from behind the bed and *bang,* the battle began. The soldiers were winning the battle. They were against the final, deadliest dinosaur. It was one vs. one. All of a sudden, *bang!* The soldiers won and they all celebrated. The dinosaurs went back into the deep dark attic and they all cried. The T-rex said, "Some day we will get revenge."

"Yeah," they all shouted.

"Get ready, boys."

Sam Swales (10)
Creigiau Primary School, Creigiau

The Story Of Darth Ted

One day, Anakin Bedwalker was playing games with his best mate Obi-Bear. "Why don't we play Exploding Kittens?" suggested Obi-Bear. Anakin Bedwalker beat Obi-Bear. Obi-Bear was not happy about this and pushed Anakin Bedwalker off the bedroom cabinet! "Aah," screamed Anakin. When he landed, he was badly hurt. Luckily he was found by a toy named Epona Plushy Face. "I can help you!" exclaimed Plushy Face. After that, Epona nursed Anakin and gave him a new look. Then his owner renamed him Darth Ted. They were happy together. His owner was very happy playing. Obi-Bear was told off.

Taliesin Campbell (10)
Creigiau Primary School, Creigiau

Angel And Devil Dolls

Smyths, at night. The dolls come alive. Angel and Devil. "Come on Angel."

"Yes, coming to clean up your mess," whispered Angel.

"Oh, look over there. The till!"

"No," shouted Angel. Suddenly, the worker came in.

"No, run," whispered Devil.

"Come over here and hide." The worker went to their boxes. How would they get back there now?

"I have a plan," cried Angel, "what if we leave, travel the world, take off?"

"Okay, let's go," shouted Devil. The dolls set off, but will they come back?

Cerys Roberts (9)
Creigiau Primary School, Creigiau

Dodo's Duty

Once there was a young, blonde, blue-eyed girl called Freya. Freya was going to the beach when she spotted a sign saying *Dodo The Dragon*. "Can I have him?" she asked.

"Okay," said Freya's mum. So she took her home after the beach.

"There you go, you sit there," Freya said. She went to have food, then a big yellow dog came in.

"Woof," barked the dog.

"Ha!" Dodo hit the dog. The battle went on, but then Freya came back with a shiny crown and walked over and put it on... the king! Dodo the fluffy king!

Freya Wetherall (10)
Creigiau Primary School, Creigiau

The Disaster In The Bedroom

One morning, the toys woke up and started to play. "It's the morning that the cleaner comes in," Lamborghini told everyone. "Oh no, here she comes, she's got the vacuum."
"Come on everyone, let's hide!"
"Oh no, Lamborghini has gone up the vacuum," Teddy told everyone. It was a bumpy ride down the stairs. Luckily, she emptied the dust into the bin. She left the lid up so the car managed to escape, but he couldn't get up the stairs. The boy walked in, saw him and carried him up and started to play with him.

Josh Barton (10)
Creigiau Primary School, Creigiau

Mission Of War

"Sergeant, the coast is clear."
"Have you got the sleeping pills for the dog?" said the sergeant.
"Yes," said the soldier.
"Move out, go." The soldiers crept across the floor and threw the pill into the dog's mouth. Suddenly, he woke up and saw the rats, then went back to sleep. The soldiers saw the rats and screamed. The dog woke up and the soldiers realised they had given the dog an energy pill. The dog went crazy. The dog saw the toy soldiers and ran as fast as he could and swallowed the soldiers.

Leo Rees (10)
Creigiau Primary School, Creigiau

My Little Pony

A pony appeared in my house, so I followed it to see where it was going. I ended up in my friend's house. She came up to me and the pony and said, "A pony!"

"I have a pony, they can be friends," I said.

"It is not my pony!" she said.

"It does not matter, you can keep that one," I said.

"No! I am taking her to her home, her family," my friend said.

"Ponies do not have families, so keep her."

"Okay, I will and I will call her Pinky." We had lots of fun!

Coco Williams (9)
Creigiau Primary School, Creigiau

Unicorn Escape

Once, there was a pink toy unicorn. She wanted to go into the sunshine. All she had to do was sneak past everyone. Although she was very big, she didn't know Unicat had followed her. "Okay," said Unicorn, "we need to get past the dog." They were doing so well until Unicat dropped her magical star and the dog woke up! Unicorn and Unicat put a spell on the dog and ran to the back door. Unicat cast the wrong spell! Unicorn fixed the spell and the dog went to sleep. Suddenly, the owner came home. They said, "Oh no!"

Lucia Andrews (9)
Creigiau Primary School, Creigiau

Sad Life Of Miss Dolphin!

The bear looked out of the bedroom door. "Okay, it is all clear," she said. Miss Dolphin fell off the bed and there was a bang! Then the boy came upstairs and accidentally squished all the toys except Miss Dolphin. The boy said, "Oops!" Miss Dolphin was crying. Then the boy ran down the stairs. Miss Dolphin packed up her stuff and grabbed her special stickers and said goodbye to her sad friends. She jumped out the window and found a new home. She played happily ever after and her new owner even had a tea party!

Lauren Smith (9)
Creigiau Primary School, Creigiau

Teddy Sam

Once, there was a teddy called Sam. Sam would come alive when no one was in the room. One day, his owner left the room and Sam came alive. Sam crept up from under the bed and walked across the messy floor to the old toy box. Sam played with the other toys that came alive. Then he played chess and Twister. Then the toy soldiers marched across the floor, followed by tanks, army jeeps and helicopters. Suddenly, Sam's owner came in. But just before the door opened, the army helicopter fell out of the sky and the toys stopped.

Tom Blake (10)
Creigiau Primary School, Creigiau

A Cow And A Tornado!

Once upon a time, there was a toy cow. He crept out of the bed and checked there weren't any people around. He had a walk around. Without him knowing, he tripped and accidentally turned the giant fan on. The fan acted like a gargantuan tornado. Slowly, the cow got sucked into the fan. Just as that was happening, the boy woke up. He wondered who turned his loud fan on. He tiptoed across the small messy room. He kept looking and looking, around and around. About two minutes later he came across a toy box. The cow was gone!

Kaitlyn Mair Halsall (10)
Creigiau Primary School, Creigiau

The Unicorn That Can't Fly

As the girl closed the door, her stuffed unicorns came to life and they started to fly about. One unicorn called Cutie couldn't fly. She went to her unicorn friends and asked them how they did it. They said, "I just think about flying and I do it." So she tried and tried but she couldn't do it. She went and asked someone else and they said the same. So she tried and tried and tried. She went to ask the other unicorns. They just said the same thing over and over again. The she tried again and did it!

Courtney Topping-Morris (10)
Creigiau Primary School, Creigiau

Snapping Soldiers War

It was a cold night in Cardiff. In a bedroom, the soldiers eyed up their target, the human, to see if they were awake so they could have a battle with their rivals. The human turned off the light. *Ching, ching!* May the battle commence. As it got further in, it got more intense. The UK were beating the US, until a big dark shadow opened the door. It flew open and the light flickered on. The soldiers were left on the floor and the human swooped down and grabbed them and snapped the soldiers into pieces.

Charlie Cartwright (10)
Creigiau Primary School, Creigiau

The Miniature Lion

The miniature lion waited for everyone to leave the garden. He played in a tiny tree, then he fell out of the tree. He slowly crept around and then saw something that looked exactly like him. He got really excited and jumped and leapt all over the place because he thought it was his brother. The toy lion jumped up and down in the long grass. When he got there, he found all of his family. They were leaping and bouncing because they had not seen him in about a year. They were so pleased and happy to see him.

Emily Blake (10)
Creigiau Primary School, Creigiau

Monkey Goes Tea Potty

Coconut was left in the garden. He decided to swing in the trees after he had had a tea party with the birds. He tried to teach the birds to swing in the trees but he failed. So Coconut tried to teach the squirrels to climb trees, but they were already experts! After, Coconut went for a jog around the garden. After five laps he had a break and then ran some more, but tripped over a twig and fell into a hole! Jimmy, his owner, called Coconut but he could not find him. Jimmy was sad and missed Coconut.

Will Lewis (10)
Creigiau Primary School, Creigiau

The Glitteratti Dolls Disappear

Once, there was a box full of L.O.L. dolls with glitter dolls inside. One day, two dolls went into Smyths and saw all the balls were gone! They checked the security cameras and saw a red thing by the box of L.O.Ls. The next day, they zoomed in on the security cameras and saw that there was a series two L.O.L. doll called Spice who took them. That night, when Spice was in bed, they went into Spice's house and took the L.O.Ls back. After that, Spice was never seen again, not even in a L.O.L. ball.

Ellie Prosser (9)
Creigiau Primary School, Creigiau

Captain Went Missing

Once upon a time, in a very dark toy box, there was a bunch of toys. They woke up but Captain was missing. That morning, they looked everywhere but still could not find him. Captain had never been missing before. They found he had fallen out of the window and into a bush. When the boy came back in with Captain they all celebrated, but his body had come off. Then they found it by the side of the bed and welcomed him back into the team. He was still a very proud and strong captain.

Max Jones (9)
Creigiau Primary School, Creigiau

Abandoned

I was stuck in an attic for a while until a human found me and this is my story. I was abandoned in a shop but it was turned into a house. I was there for two years, but I found a chest with batteries in. Yes! I plugged them into me so I could be strong. I jumped up and down causing a racket and then a human came. "Freeze!" He picked me up and brought me to a collectible stand. An earthquake hit, so to protect me, I got put into the attic and here I am now.

Sam Scott (10)
Creigiau Primary School, Creigiau

Curious Cuddle Thief

"Hi, I'm Tom and this is a story about an unwanted toy that steals the powers from my toys."
I was getting dressed for school when I heard a sparkling sound coming from the toy box...
In the box there was a very old bear that I had never seen before. He stared at me suspiciously. He was holding a big wand. I saw him steal the cuddly powers from my best teddies and I slowly started to cry. "Oh I want to cuddle my teddies," sobbed Tom.
All of a sudden, Tom's toys started rushing for my outstretched arms.

Verity Després-Davies (9)
Hafren Junior School, Newtown

That's Magic!

Jonny was sad, his mum tried to cheer him up by buying him a toy. He noticed a toy monkey sat in the toyshop window that looked sad but almost magical, so they bought it. At bedtime, just before Jonny fell asleep, the toy made a funny sound and then *whoosh*. They were in another land. They played and made new friends on lots of different adventures. They were both happy again. When Jonny awoke the monkey had gone, in its place was a teddy bear. Jonny thought it must've been just a dream but was it? That's magic!

Jessie Roberts (9)
Hafren Junior School, Newtown

Saving Bob

It was a Saturday afternoon and the toys were relaxing, until they heard a scream. It was Bob the teddy. He had managed to get up on the windowsill and he couldn't get down. "Quick, we have to stand on top of each other so I can get Bob down," shouted Barbie to all the other toys. This sounded like a good idea, there was only one problem, Mabel the marble was at the bottom of the tower. When she heard footsteps coming upstairs, she rolled away and all the toys landed in a heap on the floor.

Grace Cia Evans (9)
Hafren Junior School, Newtown

Toy Life

One sunny day, a girl named Summer was playing with her toys in her back garden. "Summer, come and have your lunch!" called Mum.

"Coming Mummy!" Summer stumbled quickly into the kitchen. The kitchen door slammed shut. Suddenly, a rubber toy dolphin started flapping around, trying to get to the pool. Then a fluffy teddy unicorn started prancing around. Little soldiers started walking. Finally, the dolphin reached the water and was splashing around! "Come on soldiers!" The unicorn was jumping with excitement. "Look, a lollipop!" Suddenly, everyone panicked as Summer stepped out the door and screamed really loudly.

Daisy Thomas (10)
Halfway Primary School, Llanelli

Toy Escape

"We've got to get out of here, I hate getting changed into different clothes!"

"Barbie has a point, we can all ride the unicorn. Let's go and get changed into brave clothes."

"Can you hear something? It cannot be Zara, she has gone out, it must be the cat. Okay, let's start getting ready. We need food as well as water, do not forget that."

Two minutes later. "We are ready." Suddenly, someone entered the room.

"Zara, what are your dolls doing on the bed? I did not put them there?" She put the toys back in the box.

Lara Louise Staples (10)

Halfway Primary School, Llanelli

Best Birthday (Not!)

One beautiful day, a girl called Ashley was so excited because it was her birthday tomorrow! She was going to get the best and cutest toy puppy. She could not wait! She suddenly fell asleep... when she woke up she shouted, "It's my birthday! I can't wait until my parents go to Smyths Toys Superstores to buy that toy puppy, but I have to stay with my annoying gran! She talks too much!" After her gran's big talk, she went home to open her presents! When she opened her toy puppy, it suddenly dropped and broke! "Ashley, no!"

Julia Murawska (9)
Halfway Primary School, Llanelli

The Ruined Party

One day, a girl called Brooklyn bought a new doll and named her Jesse. They had a great time together. They went everywhere together. Then one night, Brooklyn went downstairs and what she saw was very surprising! She saw her doll eating the birthday cake for her brother's birthday party the next day. It was a mess. All the party decorations were ruined and now they had no cake either. Her brother would be so, so sad. Now he would not be having a birthday party. She went upstairs, grabbed her coat and bought new decorations.

Bella Gilbert (10)
Halfway Primary School, Llanelli

What My Teddy Does At Night

One night, the family went out for food and the little girl left her teddy. She was very hungry so she went downstairs. She saw all of the other toys and said, "Let's go and get some food." No one agreed. She said, "I'll just go." It took her a while and as soon as she got to the fridge, a car light flashed. "Oh no! She is coming, I need to hide quickly." They all walked in and the teddy crawled across the floor. She ran as fast as she could but the little girl saw her.

Nancy Hayes (10)
Halfway Primary School, Llanelli

The Mischievous Cars

One day there lived a boy called Jeff and he liked to play with his toy car called Bob and his other one called Timothy. Jeff was nine years old. One night, he played with Bob and fell asleep. Jeff landed on Bob, so Bob tried to get out but Jeff was heavy. Timothy tried to help. It was very hard, they wanted to escape from Jeff's house. "Help," said Bob, "please, Timothy, help. Okay, I'm out now." There was no way to get out of Jeff's house and get home.

Mason Stickland (9)
Halfway Primary School, Llanelli

The Broken Football!

A girl named Annabelle, who was very good at football, had her own football. However, she'd had it since she was three and she was now ten years old. One day, she decided that she would go out to play. She went outside, got her ball from the shed and went to her back garden to play football. She kicked the ball and tried to kick it into the goal but she kicked it too high and it went over the neighbour's fence and popped. She was very sad but her parents were very mad!

Sophie Penhaligan (10)
Halfway Primary School, Llanelli

The Vanishing Toys

One sunny day, a little girl called Amy went to a new toyshop called Sticky. As soon as she left the room, a toy pig called Gilbert came to life. Gilbert went to get his friend Sunny, a toy cat. Gilbert sat on top of the dresser. It was hard for Sunny to go up and down the dresser so they both met in the middle of the room. When they got to the middle of the room, they heard a door open. They stopped what they were doing and *poof*, gone!

Caris Smith (9)
Halfway Primary School, Llanelli

Magic Coin

Hello, my name is Oli, the toy monster. I have big eyes, wiggly hands, a small blue head and the worst long legs. Two days ago I went for a walk and the other toys were laughing their heads off, so I went back home. I found a coin on the floor so I picked it up and made a wish. I looked in the mirror and I was a cute dog. I was barking really loudly and then someone took me home as their pet forever. They loved me and fed me dog food and water.

Zuzia Kajszcarek (10)
Halfway Primary School, Llanelli

The Mystery Of The Toys And The New Teddy

Hello, my name is Teddy. I lived in a toyshop but then someone picked me up and took me home. This new house is very nice. Now they have gone out for food, I am going to play with the other toys. They said that she was telling them how excited she was to get me and they are very happy to have another toy to make their family even bigger.

We played hide-and-seek and talked all day. When she came home, we pretended to be toys again.

Brooke Bell (10)

Halfway Primary School, Llanelli

The Hungry Little Dog And His Pal Matt!

One day, there was a little boy called Matt. He had a toy dog called Fresh. He always liked playing with him. One day, Matt went to the Chinese shop. While he was gone, he put his toy dog in his toy box. After a while, the toy dog came out of the toy box and went down the stairs and into the kitchen. He spilled the milk and started eating the leftover ham! Matt came back and the dog went back up to Matt's bedroom.

Maddison Ann Morris (9)

Halfway Primary School, Llanelli

The New Filly

Rose was trying to decide which one of her toys she should take to school. Then she tripped over Stardust, her toy pony who had recently given birth to a new filly.

"I know who I'm taking, Mum!" shouted Rose, scooping up the filly.

"She's adorable!" cried Rose's friends when Rose showed them.

"Can I leave her with you?" asked Rose, giving the filly to her friends. But when she returned they had lost the filly! And can you guess where they found her? In the canteen, nibbling a Galaxy bar!

"Well, her name will have to be Galaxy!"

Eva Rose Darlington Douglas (9)
Hook CP School, Hook

My Skylanders (Stealth Elf And Lightning Rod's Adventure)

"Hey, over there," said Lightning Rod.
"There's the portal to the video game," said Stealth Elf. They both jumped into the game. "Yippie," shouted the Skylanders. They were back in the game with the pretty worlds. "Uh-oh." Enemies approached. "Get ready to fight, Stealth Elf," said Lightening Rod. *Boom, smash, thwip, thwap.* The gate finally opened. "No, not the giant. He's going to chase us, run!" said Stealth Elf. They ran two miles with fright on their faces. "Quick, get on the ship," said Lightning Rod. They got on the ship with their trusty driver Kippa.

Kenneth Evans (9)
Llansawel Primary School, Briton Ferry

The Legendary Friend Escape

Once upon a time, there was a girl called Shadow. She was a doll. Shadow lived in a toy forest but she was lost. The forest was like a maze and she was trying to get to the middle. Suddenly, she bumped into another doll. Shadow told the other doll her name. The other doll's name was Owlette. They planned to escape. Shadow flew over with Owlette. Lucy came back from shopping so Shadow and Owlette froze. Then Lucy went to sleep so Shadow and Owlette escaped through a window; they ran and ran until they got home...

Chloe Lucia Rees (10) & Jessica
Llansawel Primary School, Briton Ferry

Lego Lord

Once upon a time, there was a Lego lord who ruled the land. He was a nasty lord, he treated people like they were worthless. He had slaves who got him everything. But one say, a slave stood up to the evil Lego lord. He didn't like it so he sentenced him to death, but his army didn't kill the slave. Instead, they turned against the Lego lord and pointed their swords towards him and captured him. They threw him in prison and everyone lived happily ever after.

Ieuan Evans (11)
Llansawel Primary School, Briton Ferry

A One-Armed Ranger

Once, on a very hot day, Adam and Jonathon were on the beach with their friends. Then Jonathon and his friends went over to the sea. Then Jonathon called Adam over to help him because a great white shark had started to go after him and his friends. Adam went over, but as he was walking across to him, he suddenly turned into a big huge Power Ranger and then the shark bit off one of Adam's arms. So then Adam punched it in the nose and they all went back home.

Kimberley Fowler (11)
Llansawel Primary School, Briton Ferry

The Missing Toy

"Ready or not, here I come." In Andy's room, the toys were playing hide-and-seek. Woody was on it. "Found you," he shouted. Everyone was found except Rex.
"Oh no," gasped Mrs Potato Head, "He's... missing."
"We need a plan," said Woody. "Soldier One, downstairs. Two, on the landing. Everyone, follow me."
The toys set out to find Rex.
"Woody, I repeat, Woody," said Soldier One, "found him." The toys made it downstairs.
"What were you thinking Rex?" said Woody.
"I couldn't see anyone so I hid here."
Woody looked confused and whispered, "Yes but why are you in a tutu?"

Ejiroghene Divine Adu (10)
Llantarnam Community Primary School, Cwmbran

Toy Fight: The Fluffy Monster

Litten used ember! Popplio used bubble! Rowlet used leaf storm! Then the monster hissed, scratched and tried to bite them. "Rowlet, dodge to the left!" commanded Litten. "And Popplio, distract it!" So Rowlet flew to the left and Popplio jumped onto the monster. The monster rolled onto its back and crushed Popplio. "Popplio, no!" cried Rowlet. She was so angry. She started to unleash super-powered attacks. The monster scratched and bit, but they just dodged and attacked. After what seemed like forever, the monster retreated into the bushes. "Let's leave Popplio," suggested Litten, "nobody cared about him anyway."

Alan Yang (9)
Llantarnam Community Primary School, Cwmbran

The Escape Of The Toys

"Squishy, go and check if the coast is clear," whispered Woody.

"The coast is clear boss," shouted Squishy.

"This is what we have been waiting for, let's go!" declared Woody.

"Yay, we're free! I can't wait to do all the things that I want to do," exclaimed Squishy.

"Thank you Woody for saving us all, you're my hero," said Mrs Fingerling. Soon after, before everyone went to live their own lives, Baby Fingerling came up to Woody and gave him a hug.

"What's that for?" asked Woody.

"For you, because you're my hero." Now isn't that nice?

Rachael Rich (10)

Llantarnam Community Primary School, Cwmbran

The Curious Bunny

Once, there lived a little girl called Aimee. She loved playing with her toys, but her favourite toy of all was her bunny. One day when Aimee was playing with Bunny, she heard a voice. It sounded like it was coming from Bunny's mouth! *It can't be*, Aimee thought. But suddenly, Bunny gave Aimee a wink. Aimee froze in shock. Later on that evening, when Aimee went to bed, she was thinking all about what happened that day. "I must just be having a bad dream," whispered Aimee to herself. From that day on, Bunny was never seen moving again.

Siân Fowler (10)
Llantarnam Community Primary School, Cwmbran

The Battle Of The Pacific

Once in South America, there were two toy pirate ships. They were enemies! One ship carried the Devils, the other carried the Troopers. One day, the Troopers travelled to the Pacific Ocean to find treasure! One of the Troopers saw the Devils approaching. They started shooting cannonballs at each other. Both ships sank quickly. Everyone started to jump into the ocean and swam to the nearest island. Unfortunately, the pirates swam to the same island, so the enemies continued fighting until they realised they should be friends. They built a new toy ship together.

Thomas Clark (9)

Llantarnam Community Primary School, Cwmbran

Llama In Pyjamas

Bob the toy llama lived in Billy's bedroom. Billy took Bob everywhere. One night, Billy carried Bob in his nightwear to get some milk before bed. On his way back to bed, Bob fell and landed on the stairs. Later, Bob felt a wet, slobbery mouth pick him up. Bob was frightened. Bob started spitting at the dog until he was dropped. Bob was thankful. Bob made his way up the stairs to the top and said, "No prob-llama." Bob rushed to Billy's bedroom, climbed into bed and gave him the biggest, wettest, goofiest hug ever and then fell asleep.

Connah White (10)

Llantarnam Community Primary School, Cwmbran

Dorothy The Forgotten Toy

There was a tiny doll named Dorothy. A little girl called Amy found Dorothy on the pavement near her house. Amy cared for Dorothy until one night, Dorothy was dropped down the side of Amy's butterfly bed. Amy didn't bother looking for Dorothy, or so she thought. Amy looked for days, weeks and years for Dorothy, but she was nowhere to be seen. Years passed, then an old but familiar face appeared in front of Dorothy. It was Amy! But it was not just Amy, she had a little girl and a boy. Dorothy was passed down the family.

Elizabeth Louise Jacobs (10)
Llantarnam Community Primary School, Cwmbran

The Baby Detective

Once, there was a toy baby girl called Lexi. She had a huge family. First, there were her parents. Her parents were very caring and kind. She also had a big brother, Max. She loved her toy family so much, but one day her brother went missing! Her parents looked all over the store! Max's parents were scared he had been sold! The baby girl saw Max! "Maxy, Maxy," she shouted. Her parents were so relieved that she had found Max. The parents threw a huge party and all of the toys were invited.

Jyoti Rai (9)
Llantarnam Community Primary School, Cwmbran

A Magical Adventure

One day, a little girl called Ellie was at Symths Toys Superstore. Suddenly, a huge fluffy teddy bear caught her eye. She ran over to it and gave it a big hug and then she took it home. Later that day, her friend Evie came round to play. Ellie and Evie played until night. Little did they know that in the night toys come alive and have all kinds of different adventures. That night, Teddy made an amazing obstacle course in her bedroom.
The next day when Ellie woke up, her mum told her off.

Evie Bloomer (9)
Llantarnam Community Primary School, Cwmbran

Where Did You Go Teddy?

"Come on, it's bedtime. Put teddy on your bed and brush your teeth, then we will read," said Mum.

"Okay," said Hannah.

"Are you ready? We will read 'Little Red Riding Hood'," said Mum.

"Oh no!" said Hannah.

"What's wrong?" said Mum.

"Rosie's gone," said Hannah. "I can't get to sleep without her."

"Check your bed once more," said Mum.

"She's not here," said Hannah.

"Has she fallen off your bed?" said Mum.

"Found her," said Hannah.

"Okay, so are you ready for a story?" said Mum.

"Yes I am," said Hannah. "Get warm teddy, silly."

Lorna Jacobs (10)
Penarlag Primary School, Ewloe

L.O.L. Fun Time

Lucy rushed out and the door slammed loudly. "Quick Luxe, jump onto the carousel," shouted Treasure. They span round and round, up and down. "Faster, faster!" screamed Luxe.
"Woah!" Treasure shouted. Suddenly, Luxe noticed a shadow. It got really big.
"Quick Treasure, back in our box," whispered Luxe. They ran as fast as they could. Lucy had forgotten her school bag. She quickly scooped up her favourite toys. "That was close," said Luxe.
"Yes, but it was fun," Treasure said mischievously. They both sat in the darkness of Lucy's bag, awaiting the next golden school time adventure.

Lucy Elizabeth Davies (8)
Penarlag Primary School, Ewloe

The Doll

In the school library, Lucy said, "Let's go to Emma's house." So they all went to Emma's house. They made it spooky, very spooky. Lucy ran and put spooky music on Emma's rainbow CD player, Meg put blankets everywhere and Emma put the fan on. They pretended they were visiting a haunted house and explored the house. Up in Emma's room, the door suddenly creaked open. The three girls noticed Emma's favourite doll from Jamaica was moving. It was talking. The girls screamed and ran down the stairs, flying out of the door. They ran to Lucy's safe, warm home.

Lily Burnett (9)
Penarlag Primary School, Ewloe

A Table Footballer's Dream

"What does it look like? Tell us! Tell us!" The table football away team were impatient and frustrated because the home team could see out of the conservatory window into the garden. "Well..." smiled the home team captain, "it's green and looks amazing!" All they had ever dreamed of was to play on grass outside in the fresh air, instead of being spun around at a vast rate of knots. The goalkeepers were still feeling dizzy from this morning's game. They had to think of a way to escape. But first things first... how could they get off the poles?

Lillia Grace James (10)
Penarlag Primary School, Ewloe

Midnight's Story

"It's tight in here," I bellowed. *Crack!* Light filled the plastic ball as Isabel tore open the packet. I hadn't seen this much light since I'd been created in the L.O.L. factory. I was naked but Isabel dressed me. "Kids, it's time to go," shouted Isabel's mum. I was carried out of the door in a dark bag. The car made me feel sick! They forgot all about me for months. I screamed, but they didn't hear me. Suddenly, Isabel's dad tipped his bag out. Daylight!

Molly Catherine Dathan (9)
Penarlag Primary School, Ewloe

Shopkins Adventure

Once upon a time, there lived lots of Shopkins. One of them was called Buncho Bananas. They lived in a big cottage, but Buncho Bananas went on an adventure. Buncho Bananas saw a little girl in a little house. Then Buncho Bananas heard her shout something from the window, "What is that?" she asked. Buncho Bananas went up to the little girl and the Shopkin went into the little girl's window. "Are you a Shopkin?" she asked him. Then they became best friends forever.

Phoebe Wright (10)

Penarlag Primary School, Ewloe

The Jumping Pig

Once upon a time, there lived a toy pig called Momo. He was very good at jumping so he decided to go to the Olympics. First, he went on the trampoline. He jumped as high as he could and won a trophy. He was so worn out he decided to drive all the way home. When he got home, he sat on the couch and said, "Ah, this is nice." He went into the kitchen and got nice biscuits and sat down on some cushions.

Faye Allonby (9)
Penarlag Primary School, Ewloe

Future Alfie

I was sat in my bedroom when Future Alfie warned me, "Quick, there's someone coming up the stairs, it's your mum." We needed to tidy up and put everyone in their positions so nobody would be suspicious. They didn't need to know what we were planning. "Great, they're gone, let's sort this mission out."

"We need to find out where the toys are going. I suspect it's Harri."

"We need to get into his bedroom without him knowing."

"Let's go. They're in there, in his bedroom!"

"Get them all out quickly."

"Well done boys, all safe in my bedroom."

Alfie George Griffiths (9)
Sandycroft Primary School, Mancot

Amelia's Amazing Adventure

"I'm Barbie. I'm Ken," Amelia said as she put on a fake voice.

"Amelia, breakfast's ready," Amelia's mum shouted. Amelia rushed down to have a yummy breakfast with her family. "We can move now," Barbie whispered to Ken. *Tap, tap, tap* went the tiny footsteps of Barbie and Ken walking towards the house. Amelia walked in to find her Barbies walking across the bedroom floor. "OMG," Amelia shrieked. As soon as Amelia had said that, she shrunk down to Barbie size. "Hi, I think you know who we are."

"Yeah," Amelia said. They hopped in the car and drove off...

Lilly Gibson-Taylor (9)
Sandycroft Primary School, Mancot

Cutie's Lucky Escape

"Aargh!" shouted Cutie as she landed on the grass, falling from Kacey's basket on her bike. "Oh no! I'm lost," said Cutie, seeing Kacey pedal off. Cutie was scared. "I need to find Kacey! What am I going to do?" shouted Cutie. "Help!" screamed Cutie, running through the grass, not knowing where she was going. Seconds felt like hours. Cutie felt a gust of wind. "Oh no! What's that? Chance our dog!" Cutie grabbed onto his tail. "Woohoo!" screamed Cutie, speeding through the grass. Cutie let go, spinning in the air, landing back in Kacey's basket. Now that was lucky!

Kacey Summer Nelson (7)
Sandycroft Primary School, Mancot

Barbie Playtime

"Let's have fun while Aimee's asleep."

"Yes, let's party Barbie and have some fun."

"The pool is still set up from before and the cars are still here. So we can drive round the bedroom then take a dip in the pool. No splashing though, because Aimee may wake up."

"If only she knew what we get up to while she's asleep."

"So much fun she's missing out on. It's a shame really."

"Whoops, the carpet is soaked."

"Aimee will get the blame."

"Let's clean up the best we can ready for tomorrow."

Aimee Butler (8)
Sandycroft Primary School, Mancot

My Magical Unicorn

Sarah's mum is in the garden working with the flowers. She asks Sarah, "Would you mind going into the forest to collect some berries? We could make a cherry pie for pudding."
Sarah collects a basket and skips off singing. When she enters the forest, she spots something shiny. When she looks up she sees it's a unicorn. "Wow!" says Sarah.
"Hi," says Shimmer. "Would you like to go with me on an adventure?"
"With you? Yes please," says Sarah, and off they go on an adventure.
When they come back home Sarah says, "I will never forget you."

Scarlett Joanna Davies (8)
Sandycroft Primary School, Mancot

Doll's Blog

"How did your day go?"

"Daisy took me to school with her. Daisy's friend took great care of me. I enjoyed maths. I know how to read the time and in English they told us who Shakespeare was."

"Wait, let me tell you, Tom dropped me in a puddle," said Tom's teddy.

"I met Lexi's toys," shared Martin's African monkey toy.

"Oh no! Daisy's awake! Bye, and don't forget to follow my blog!" Daisy awoke and saw the room was filled with the computer's light. When she turned around, she saw her doll sitting in her computer chair.

Silvi Ivanova (10)
Sandycroft Primary School, Mancot

I Knew My Toys Were Alive!

Out of the shadows appeared a large human-shaped figure. The partying toys didn't notice until the light switched on. All of the teddies, soldiers and every other toy dropped down. But it was too late, they had been caught. Evie had always thought that her toys were moving, but no one ever believed her. Now she had proof. "I wonder if she knows we're alive?" her favourite teddy said. "Of course she does, she's right there!" a pizza slice cushion said from the corner of Evie's bed. "She definitely knows now, shh!" Their fun with Evie was only just beginning.

Isabelle Megan Webber (10)

Sandycroft Primary School, Mancot

Toy Escape

In a bedroom, a little boy was playing with his toys. That night, they were lost so he went to investigate. Billy followed the trail, but it stopped and he found the toys. They were running away. He picked one up and said, "Where are you going, Smith?"

"Nowhere," he said.

"Look here, you're going somewhere. Right, I'll make you a deal. I'll put you down, but you stay here."

"Okay, but don't say we can talk or anything."

"Alright. Quick soldiers, move him."

"Not again," said Smith.

Sasha Jackson (8)
Sandycroft Primary School, Mancot

I Love You... To Bits!

"Oh look Fluffy, you're all dirty... it's bath time!" She stuffed her doll into the bath and clutched it hard with an evil grin on her face. "Still dirty..." she cackled. She grabbed a hairdryer from the corner and put it on full blast, making Fluffy fall over. "Let's play some more!" she howled. The little girl threw the toy into the air and whacked it with her tennis racket. She then fought over it with her friend and lastly said, "You're my best friend, do you like me too?"
"Please end this..." said Fluffy.

Lewis Bult (11)
Sandycroft Primary School, Mancot

Closed

One afternoon in Smyths toyshop, a Fingerling woke up, excited for the shop closing at 6pm. *Five more minutes to go*, she thought, *until we're all alone and all my friends wake up.* The lights went off and all of a sudden, Ken shouted, "Come on Barbie, let's go party." Teddy pressed a button and the disco ball shone brightly throughout the shop. The music was on full blast. Everyone was having a great time. The night went so quickly, it was already 7.50am. With only ten minutes to spare, they ran back to their places. The lights turned on...

Chloe Turner (11)
Sandycroft Primary School, Mancot

Blinky's Big Boom!

"I can't believe it's down to a golden goal," said Bouncer, excitedly. It was the playroom football final. In a flash, the ball sped up the pitch. Buzzy Bear, then Blitzo, with Blinky lined up by the back post just waiting for the perfect moment for their big win. *Boom!* Blinky smashed it, back of the net. The toys went wild. This was the first time in playroom history that B Team had won the Letter League. "Code Kid," shouted Blinky, and all the toys scarpered back to their boxes as the light flickered on... Charlie awoke, the toys froze.

Ossian Rhys Jones (11)
Sandycroft Primary School, Mancot

The Oliver's Bedroom Football Cup

One Monday morning, Oliver had just left for school. When Oliver left, his room fell silent. In the SoccerStarz tub, Kevin De Bruyne said, "Lads, you want a mini tournament?" So they picked the teams. Ronaldo, Messi, Neymar and KDB were all the captains. Kevin De Bruyne's team played fantastically well. KDB ended up scoring the most goals, beating Ronaldo by one. De Bruyne's team played Ronaldo's team in the final. De Bruyne's team won, eleven-nine. They all had loads of fun and had to rush to get back in the SoccerStarz tub before Oliver got home.

Oliver Gilburt (8)
Sandycroft Primary School, Mancot

Jeff's Short Trip To Earth

"Jeff, why are you so clean? You're hideously spotless," Jeff's friends giggled. He was a silly alien with sparkling green skin and three big eyes, unlike the other aliens who lived on Planet Orange; they were dirty.

Jeff was clearing up when he found a map. His eyes lit up when he found Earth. "It's so... clean!" He jumped for joy and ran to his UFO.

It took him sixty years to get there, he was excited. But when he got there it was horrible, plastic bags and rubbish everywhere. "I need to get out of here." He went home.

Hannah (7)
Sandycroft Primary School, Mancot

The Toyshop

There was a toyshop. The toys lived and played there. A gang of toys adventured around the spacious toyshop. They loved it there. Their names were Blob, Wheels, Solar and Sludge. They looked ugly, so they weren't bought for a long time. Then one day, Blob was bought by a little girl. "Let's go with Blob," Wheels yelled. So they did! Finally, they got to the girl's house.

"Psst, take us back to the shop!" the gang chorused.

"Okay." The little girl understood. They went back, she put them on their shelf and then left.

Harrison Finley Webber (8)
Sandycroft Primary School, Mancot

Two Pairs Of Eyes

In a small town lived two children called Rachel and Peter. Their favourite thing to do was play in the nursery. They thought their toys were normal, but at night something amazing happened. Their toys came alive! It was dark, the clock struck midnight. There was silence. "The coast is clear," whispered Sergeant. One by one, the toys were coming to life. Rachel's dolls, Peter's army men and lots more. The dolls set up the doll's house and they had a magnificent tea party. Suddenly, the lights switched on. All the toys saw was two pairs of eyes.

Imogen Hoyle (10)
Sandycroft Primary School, Mancot

The Woodland Adventure

"Goodnight Mum and Dad," said Rosey and Bob. They were soon fast asleep. Pink Ted and Tiger crept from the children's tent. The camp fire was still lit. The toys started toasting marshmallows on the fire. They toasted them all. They tampered with the tents and messed up the campsite. The toys walked away, silently eating marshmallows. "Mum, Dad. Ted and Tiger have gone," shouted Rosey and Bob. The family came out of their tents to find the campsite was wrecked. There was a trail of pink and white marshmallows leading off into the forest.

Carys Williams (8)
Sandycroft Primary School, Mancot

Ouija Board

One stormy night, two girls were having a sleepover. They were playing with porcelain dolls. They put the dolls on the shelf, then Kate pulled a Ouija board from under her bed. "You can't be serious," said Ellie.

"Let's play," said Kate. So they placed their fingers on the planchette and asked, "Is there a spirit in this room?" The planchette moved to the word yes. Then a chill shot down Ellie's spine. "Where are you?" said the girls. 'D O L L'. Suddenly, the doll's head turned to the left.

Paris Finney (10)
Sandycroft Primary School, Mancot

The Dream Teddy

Hi, I'm Teddy Nel. I can't wait for Livia to go to sleep tonight! I'm on a mission to go to Sofia. She's having a bad dream about scary dinosaurs. I'm going to help her! Let's catch the dinosaurs and send rainbow unicorns, Sofia loves them. All done! The mission is complete. I'm so tired, let's go back to Livia's bed before she wakes up and realises that I'm not there. She would be very sad, she's my BFF. I can't wait for my next adventure. I love this job! Shh... Livia is waking up. I need to freeze.

Nel Boryc (8)
Sandycroft Primary School, Mancot

Under The Bed

Every night, under the bed, Alice's toys get up to mischief. For instance, last night they had a party. They played hide-and-seek and built a campfire out of red, orange, yellow and brown Lego bricks. They told each other about their day with Alice. Tonight, they are planning to have theatre classes. They will be rehearsing for their famous annual toy show. This year it will be 'Oliver Twist'! But they must make sure they put everything, including themselves, away in the morning so Alice doesn't know what they've been up to.

Pema Hodgson (9)
Sandycroft Primary School, Mancot

Jay Bear's Adventure

Jay Bear's adventure began on a shelf. He was nervous and excited as he moved closer to the front of the shelf. Then all of a sudden, there he was. Jay Bear had never been so happy. His eyes widened as he hoped to become someone's best friend. A young girl called Alicia ran straight over to Jay Bear, grabbed him and yelled excitedly, "This one please Mummy." She held him so tightly. Jay Bear stayed in Alicia's arms all the way home and knew he was her best friend. Jay Bear and Alicia went on adventures together every day.

Alicia Smith (7)
Sandycroft Primary School, Mancot

The Dog Is Coming

"Green, red, blue and yellow," said a toy, while dancing around the room. Bluey was playing Twister, waiting for the... "Dog! Help me!" shouted Bluey. All the toys ran to the dog but he was too strong. Bluey was gone, they all thought, but he wasn't. "He's on the bed," said a toy. He was pretending to be dead so the dog didn't get him. "Help!" said another toy. "I'm going to be eaten." Bluey jumped in the way and was eaten by the dog! The toys all held a funeral for Bluey.

Lauren Roberts (10)

Sandycroft Primary School, Mancot

Lucky's New Friend

One day, there were two teddies playing. Their names were Sparkles and Lucky. Lucky was a blue and green dog and his friend Sparkles was a pink and green horse. They played football and played on the swings. Lucky scored the winning goal for his team. Sparkles won a trophy for the highest swing, beating the cheating monkey. Later, a snake joined them. He was new and had two horns on his head. Everyone was scared, except Lucky who went to make friends with him. His name was Longtail and soon everyone was friends with the new snake teddy.

Tashi Hodgson (7)
Sandycroft Primary School, Mancot

Life Of A Doll

She came into the room as she always did, but this time it was different. I could see her putting toys in a bag. Then a hand reached me and I heard the absolute dreaded words, "Cassie's too old for this now," said the mother. Then she went in the cold bin. It was as dark as a raven's feather. Suddenly, the silence was broken by the faint sound of arguing. "She's not being thrown away." Then the lid opened. The light blinded me. A hand reached out to me. "I'm keeping you forever, doll."

Lizzy Mills (10)
Sandycroft Primary School, Mancot

Tim And The Magic Ball

Tim was excited about his new ball given to him by his grandad. He ran into the garden and began kicking it around. Suddenly, it started to glow. Tim was so surprised, he stopped kicking it. A door appeared, coming from the ball. Curiously, Tim went through the door. As he stepped through, he saw a magical world with every toy he had ever wanted to play with. The toys were all coming to life. Tim raced over to the Huffy bike, jumped on and started pedalling around. Next, he played with the cars. Then things started to change...

Afon Fewster-Jones (11)

Sandycroft Primary School, Mancot

Revenge Of The Ragdoll

In a small town there was a charity shop. In the window sat a scruffy ragdoll. All she wanted was to have a happy life. One day, a little girl called Lucy walked past the shop with her eyes glistening. "Daddy, look at the dolly. Please can I have her?" "Of course." He bought it for her. Lucy took her everywhere. She came home from school and told the dolly she was being bullied. She also mentioned it was take your toy to school day and she was taking her. Dolly was ready to teach the bullies a lesson.

Ellie Evans (11)
Sandycroft Primary School, Mancot

Escape The Cuddle

Oh no, it's 8pm. That means it's nearly Macy's bedtime and me being her bedtime fluffy bear, means that I'm going to be so tightly squeezed that it feels like my ears are going to fall off. Oh, here she comes, get ready. Oh that's tight. Getting tighter. Tighter again. Ahhh, my ears are starting to twitch. I hope she falls asleep soon. Oh good, her eyes are finally closed. Next will come the big breath and then the start of the snoring. At last, the grip has loosened. I can go and play with the other toys.

Macy Jones (8)

Sandycroft Primary School, Mancot

Monster House

Hi, my name is Bob, I'm a demon. I'm Bill's toy. Bill is a boy and I'm his favourite toy. A couple of weeks ago, somebody died in the house across the street and now apparently the house is haunted, but I don't believe it. I have seen some paranormal activity going on in our house recently. I kind of believe it, but not 100%. But then, somebody or something started pushing me around. I don't know what it was. There was a car noise outside and five minutes later, my owner had arrived back home early.

Jayden Bentham Ryan (10)
Sandycroft Primary School, Mancot

Crispy Cream's Story

One misty morning there was a lovely unicorn called Crispy Cream. She loved being happy in her wonderful fantasy land. In her magical kingdom, her fellow people loved her so much.

One fine, crisp day she went to a waterfall. She took a sip of the water but then something bad happened, a big storm came and struck Crispy Cream.

She woke up as a little girl. She was really confused at first but then she realised it happened to all the unicorns. She wanted to be a person forever so that's what happened.

Jade Jenna Wemyss (11)
Sandycroft Primary School, Mancot

Mission To Mars!

"Is the rocket sorted?" said the astronaut. His dream was to go to Mars! He was in a toyshop. Every day he dreamt of going to Mars, with its tasty caramel centre. He had finally fixed the rocket to go to Mars. After a bumpy ride, he landed on the crinkly Mars bar wrapper. He was excited, walking over the hot, red surface. He had a tough time battling the wrapper and then fell into the delicious, sticky caramel. He ate all of the caramel and his dream had come true. He went to Mars every single day.

Cameron Gallagher (8)
Sandycroft Primary School, Mancot

The Night Before Christmas

It was the night before Christmas. Jack was asleep and the presents were wrapped and under the tree. Miniature shadows crept down the stairs and opened each present as if they were theirs. They put each new toy into the bin, making sure it was their year again. One toy felt guilty and knew it was wrong. He crept back down and put each present back under the tree. The next morning, the toy watched Jack open his presents with warmth in his heart. He went back upstairs and jumped back into Jack's toy box.

Jessica Bleasdale (11)
Sandycroft Primary School, Mancot

My Hair!

Here I am again. Oh gosh, that tiara is ripping out my hair. I'm lying on those other Barbies, but I know I won't be here for long. Oh no, here she comes. And this time she has scissors. She picks me up, her hand grasping my torso, her nails making dents in my scratched and graffitied plastic skin. She pulls the tiara out of my hair and snips the length of it off. I still have a short bob though. Wait, she's also got her dad's razor. She drags it along my scalp, getting rid of all my hair.

Tegan-Lily Ellis-Smith (10)
Sandycroft Primary School, Mancot

Teddy's Adventure

Joey and his teddy, Snuggles, went on holiday with his family to Ohio. It was so hot, the dad shouted, "Let's go to the pool!" Snuggles got left on the bed. When the maid came in to change the bed, the teddy was wrapped up in the sheets! Joey came back and saw that Snuggles was gone. What Joey didn't know was that Snuggles was a special teddy with special powers. Joey made the hotel owner's dog better and after that, they had free holidays in the hotel. He's the best teddy ever!

Imogen Bell (10)

Sandycroft Primary School, Mancot

The Magic Toyshop

One morning when Smyths toyshop was opening, a crowd of children rushed in, searching for their favourite toy aisle. A girl named Illya ran to her favourite aisle which was the one with the unicorns in it. She loved unicorns, they were so magical. She looked at all the unicorn toys but she found one that looked different from the others. It looked more... alive. She grabbed it and wished it would come to life. The second she said that, the toy changed. It was no longer a normal toy, it was breathing...

Karina Kasperek (11)
Sandycroft Primary School, Mancot

The Incredible Bear

One day, a boy named Josh heard a knock on his door. He opened the door and there was a man standing there with a big teddy bear. The man said that he wanted Josh to have the bear because he sensed a special power in him. He told Josh that the bear was very unusual because he could talk, was super strong and could shape-shift. Josh was very excited by this so he kept him and called him Bruce. As they grew older, Josh and Bruce fought crime and helped lots of people. They were called the Terrific Two!

Joseph Parry (8)
Sandycroft Primary School, Mancot

The Day Before Billy's Birthday

In Jogger's Lane, there lived a boy named Billy. Billy was twelve years old and had over fifty toys, teddies, cars and planes! He had always wished that they would come to life, but that wish never seemed to come true! Billy's birthday was tomorrow and he really wanted to play with his toys when they were alive. Suddenly, Billy heard a sound that sounded like a car! He soon found one of his cars driving itself round a track whilst speaking to the other cars. What would happen next?

Rhieyen Emily Anne Jones (11)

Sandycroft Primary School, Mancot

A Day In The Life Of Barbie

Dear Diary,

Today when I woke up, I felt a bit stiff. Then I put my favourite dress on and went downstairs to have waffles for breakfast. Then my phone rang. I picked it up and it was my friend Chelsea ringing. She asked if we could meet up at the mall in ten minutes. I said yes, so off we went! We had a coffee, then spent all of our money on dresses. I checked my phone, it was teatime. Chelsea came for dinner and a sleepover. We had lots of fun, it was fantastic!

Love, Barbie!

Abigail Paterson (8)

Sandycroft Primary School, Mancot

A Mind-Blowing Day

The bell rang, it was playtime for all the young kids in the school. There was one little girl called Amy. She was the only child who didn't really enjoy playtime because she had to leave the toys for thirty long minutes. Of course, she huffed and puffed, but eventually left the toys. As soon as all the children left the building, there were tiny little voices around the room. The toys had come to life! There were dozens, but their leader was a little fairy called Molly Pixie.

Ella Ford (10)
Sandycroft Primary School, Mancot

The Little Doll Who Loved Adventures

Once upon a time, there was a toy store. The workers made a doll called Little Mia. Little Mia wanted to look around the toy store. One night, an evil doll, who was black and white, made everything black and white. When Little Mia saw everything black and white, she touched it and turned it into beautiful, bright colours. Little Mia saved the day. Every doll loved her and so a few days later, all the nice dolls got an owner. So did Little Mia. They all lived happily ever after.

Mia Jasmontaite (8)
Sandycroft Primary School, Mancot

The Missing Tail

One day, a girl called Sarah had a new dinosaur toy. They went to the park. After a few hours, they went back home, but her toy's tail was missing. Sarah asked her mum to look for the toy, but it was getting dark and sadly Sarah had to go to bed. The next morning, Sarah wanted to find her toy's tail. Firstly, she looked under her bed but remembered that she had gone to the park. So she went to the park and found the tail in the bush. She was so happy she had found it.

Caitlyn Jones (8)
Sandycroft Primary School, Mancot

The Little Unicorn

Once upon a time, there was a little unicorn who lived in a rainbow castle. She loved where she lived, but she lived alone so she was sad. However, she had lots of friends who she cared for. She always played with them. Their names were Lily, Holly, Ruby and Summer. Her name was Shine because she was covered in glitter! They were all toys who could come to life. They never broke up! Holly was a cheetah, Lily was a pony, Summer was a butterfly and Ruby was a hummingbird.

Sara Soghier (8)
Sandycroft Primary School, Mancot

Wash Day Escape

"The coast is clear Vanilla Bear!" shouted Mia Ballerina.

"Attention all fluffy friends! This is our chance to escape from the imminent threat! Follow me!" roared Vanilla, clumsily trying to clamber out of the dangerously deep laundry basket.

"Speed up Vanilla, your fluffy bum-bum is in my way!" shouted Ginger the cat, prodding a claw at Vanilla's bottom.

"Don't forget about me," lamented White Rabbit. "I don't want to be whirled together with some smelly socks; I respect myself." Mia Ballerina, hearing the commotion within, leapt to the basket. Then, a crash! The basket toppled. "We're free!" cheered everyone.

Evelina Lawrence (7)
St Joseph's Primary School, Gabalfa

The Tedicorn

One day, Ryan was playing with Buster the unicorn toy. Ryan loved Buster because he was cute, but then Benji came along. Buster was cute and all, but Benji was amazing. Buster was fed up of everything being about Benji, so he said to Ally, the puppy toy, "Let's get revenge."
Ally said, "That sounds mean."

"Who cares?" said Buster. Then he said to Benji, "Ryan doesn't like you really, he's just trying to make you feel better because you're ugly."
Ally said, "Um, yeah." Benji was upset, but Benji explained that they were from the same store. BFFs.

Ruby Morgan Spain (8)
St Joseph's Primary School, Gabalfa

The Dark Mystery

In a fun place called Llangrannog, three toys named Mr Boo, Tyler and Snuggles lived. They decided that morning that they would go to explore the woods. When they set out they had a nice picnic. "Shom shoom shopa loopa," said Mr Boo in his language. When Tyler went to the bin to put his rubbish in, he fell asleep and without him noticing, a UFO lifted him up. That was a mystery! The two went on without him, but they were lost. Snuggles went away and a killer took her. She was never seen again. Mr Boo went home.

Nandana Suresh (7)
St Joseph's Primary School, Gabalfa

The Great Adventure

Once, my action figure came alive while we were on holiday. He got up! The house was like a massive mansion for the action figure because he was so small. He saw a cat flap in the door and he went out. He saw what he thought was a monster, but it was just my cat. It chased him. He ran into a tree, he was safe. He saw loads of bugs, he had a little talk. He ran back into the house. The cat got stuck. He fell asleep and dreamt of the most fantastic day ever!

Jamie Dafydd Nott (7)
St Joseph's Primary School, Gabalfa

Her Dream Came True

One day, a girl called Lila was daydreaming about having a toy that was a small electric car. She stayed in her bed for twenty-four hours thinking of the colour of the car, the power of the car and where she should play with the car. It would be purple and shiny, a two-seater and the power would be 40CC.

Suddenly, she got out of bed and was sad because her parents couldn't afford it. Then her mum said, "Your friend is coming over for a beautiful party."
Knock, knock!
"Lila, look down!" Her dream had come true!

Hana Dualeh (8)
Ummul Mumineen Academy, Grangetown

Toy Terror

"Toys are not real!" shouted my brother as he stormed out of the room.
"Who does he think he is?" said Maryam angrily. "We can walk, we can talk and we can eat." Maryam was always angry if her family were insulted. She had a really bad temper. "We could pull a trick on him," said Philip the Prankster, "we could steal his belongings and return them later." The next day, the plan was carried out. One minute Adam had his pencil case, the next minute, we heard a piercing scream. He was angry...

Humayra Arish (9)
Ummul Mumineen Academy, Grangetown

Where's Ducky?

"Where's he gone now?" said Mummy Duck, while the other ducks played together.

"Who, Mummy?" said Happy Duck.

"Dopey, your little brother," replied Mummy who sounded tired.

"Quick, everyone keep still, the human is coming," said another bath toy, in fear as a human came to turn on the shiny tap that immediately ran water into the bath.

"Happy, look under the flannels by the taps," said Mummy furiously. "Grumpy, look by the bottles and I will look in the bubbles."

"Dopey?" came voices from everywhere, when suddenly a bold little purple head popped up.

"Hello," came a voice.

"Dopey!"

Jessica Jenkins (11)
Waunarlwydd Primary School, Waunarlwydd

Toy Time!

"Okay!" said Drew. "Let's work this out!"
"Let's climb!" screeched Pyramid Man. So all the toys climbed out of the cramped, dusty, scorching toy box. As Drew led the way, Pyramid Man pressed a button saying 'OMG!' Then a loud buzz started, leaving their plastic eardrums ringing. "Bad idea," muttered Drew. There was a loud banging and the door opened. A terrifying monster came in. "Uh-oh..." whispered Drew. Then the monster began banging and stomping. "Run!" shouted Pyramid Man. Then they realised it was just the goofy little sister! "Phew," said Pyramid Man.
"I know right?" said Drew, laughing.

Kian Lehane (10)
Waunarlwydd Primary School, Waunarlwydd

Smash And Crash!

"Wee," screeched Tim the plane, flying higher and higher around the bedroom. Suddenly, there was a huge crash! "Oh no, Percy Piggybank is smashed," yelled Tim! "What do we do?"
"Don't worry," said Bob Builder Teddy, "I'll fix it." He happily got to work, sticking and gluing. He was done in no time. "Why isn't Percy talking?" asked Tim anxiously.
"Hmm," said Bob, "I wonder." He glanced at the scattered coins on the floor. "I know," he said. He dropped a few coins into Percy and waited.
"You saved my life," Percy exclaimed. "Thank you everyone," he said happily.

Ella Harris (9)
Waunarlwydd Primary School, Waunarlwydd

The Lonely Lego

"I wish I had a friend!" sighed Jeffrey. For too long, Jeffrey had been a sad, lonely Lego piece. He was the last Lego piece in Kirsty's toy box. Jeffrey heard noises - Ruth, Kirsty's best friend, had come to play. "Go on!" giggled Ruth, "Let's swap." With a clunk, a little yellow square fell into the toy box, in place of Robbie the rubber. Jeffrey looked nervously at this new yellow thing! "Hello, I'm Maddie!" said the little yellow piece of Lego. "Wow!" spluttered Jeffrey. "You're Lego like me!" They both smiled. Jeffrey wasn't lonely anymore.

Bailey Lewis (10)
Waunarlwydd Primary School, Waunarlwydd

Slippy Tracks

Bleep! They're off! Furious Finn leads, ahead of Dexterous Dan, while Skidding Stu struggles to keep up. The racers approach the titanic Lego house, swerving to evade the ostentatious furniture. Looks like Finn has had an early crash! Stu has caught up and is now leading! Next up, the windowpane. Stu and Dan drift over its moist stickers, slipping and sliding! "Got yourself in a sticky situation, Stu?"
"I'm not the one with chewing gum tyres, Dan!" They fly over the pillow ramp, through the Morpurgo book tunnel and Stu crosses the finish line! "Aah!" Giant hands close in...

Matthew James (11)
Waunarlwydd Primary School, Waunarlwydd

Surprise! Squidgy Ball

"Please let me be a Christmas present," whispered Squidgy, the small red sponge ball. Suddenly, an escaped dog burst into the toyshop, grabbed Squidgy in his slimy, drooling mouth and ran away. "You're hurting me," cried Squidgy.
"Come back," yelled a boy. Squidgy dropped out, lost and sad. The night became dark and frightening. Shivering, Squidgy heard bells and saw a light in the sky. A sleigh full of presents landed. Someone lifted Squidgy and put him onto a reindeer's cold blue nose. The sleigh zoomed like a rocket into the frosty sky. Squidgy was glowing red with happiness.

Emily Evans (9)
Waunarlwydd Primary School, Waunarlwydd

Plastic

"Mum, can I have it?"
"No, it's only plastic."
"Dad, can I have a new toy?"
"Really, it's just plastic."
We've got feelings, plastic. We're not just toys.
Don't leave us on the shelf because once in a
while, we all enjoy a little fun, even when we're not
in the best of moods! Take a look, have some fun.
But if you don't like us, take us to the charity shop.
Another child would appreciate a new piece of
plastic. Think about happiness, it could do you
some good. Not all plastic items are the harmful
kind. Reconsider plastic.

Ruby Oliver (11)
Waunarlwydd Primary School, Waunarlwydd

The Magical Unicorn

In a girl's bedroom lived a magical toy unicorn called Sparkle. Every night when the girl gets sleepy, Sparkle comes alive. Sparkle goes out and grants dreams and wishes to every child. One night, Sparkle got lost. "If only I knew the way home," Sparkle thought. She spotted Twinkle, the Tooth Fairy, fluttering out of an open window. "Can you help me find my way home Twinkle?" Sparkle begged.

"Of course," Twinkle replied. After flying for a while, they noticed the street below and said goodbye. "Ah, home sweet home." Moments later, the girl awoke.

Hattie Hughes (10)
Waunarlwydd Primary School, Waunarlwydd

Friends

There once was a toy duck called Jeffrey. He lived in a toy house on his own. Jeffrey got lonely at times and wanted a friend. One day, Jeffrey went to the park. It was very quiet. There was one little toy mouse playing on the slide. Jeffrey went over to the mouse. "Hello," said Jeffrey, "what's your name?"

"Bobby," replied the mouse, "would you like to play?" Jeffrey smiled and they began to play. Jeffrey didn't feel lonely anymore. Bobby and Jeffrey became best friends and met at the park every day to play. They lived happily ever after.

Tyler Penherwood (11)
Waunarlwydd Primary School, Waunarlwydd

Lewis, Tidy Your Room

"Lewis, tidy your bedroom!" my mum shouted. "No Xbox until it's done."

I stood looking at the mess on my floor and remembered a film I'd seen at Christmas. I clicked my fingers and watched with amazement as Buzz flew up onto his shelf, followed by Woody who bungeed up on his pull cord. Another click and my RC cars turned double doughnuts and parked neatly under my bed. The huge pile of Lego leapt into the crate, which slid under my bed.

Mum came in and looked amazed. "Wow Lewis, an extra fifteen minutes of Xbox time for you."

Lewis William Rees (9)
Waunarlwydd Primary School, Waunarlwydd

Police Boy

Joey went to the toy store to spend his birthday money. "That's the one!" Joey exclaimed. On returning home, Joey ran to his room where he played with his new toy. "I wish I was a real policeman," he said. All of a sudden, his toy came to life. "You can be," said his little toy. Joey was astonished.
"You just spoke, how?"
"I heard you wishing to be a real policeman and I wanted to tell you that your wish can come true if you believe in yourself and work hard in school. You can become the best policeman."

Lily Marie Thomas (10)
Waunarlwydd Primary School, Waunarlwydd

Always Accept Everyone!

Once, there was a toy bunny called Brooke who had a best friend, Milly the mouse. They were the best of friends. They would have sleepovers and do lots of fun things together. But one day, Milly met a new friend and hardly ever played with Brooke. So one day, Brooke said to Milly, "Can I join in because I'm your best friend and you've been leaving me out!"

"Sorry," said Milly, "of course you can, this is Percy the pig!"

"Hi," said Percy.

"Hi," said Brooke. Then they all played together as BFFs.

Daisy Mansell (11)

Waunarlwydd Primary School, Waunarlwydd

The Adventures Of Baby Shrek

"Ahh!" baby Shrek opened his eyes and reached out to feel for his favourite toy, Maximilion. Instead of feeling the soft fur of Max, he felt nothing! As his sleepy eyes focused on the bedroom door, to his horror, he saw the legs of Max hanging from his dog Rufus' slobbery mouth. He knew he needed to act quickly. He jumped from his bed and sprinted to the door. "I'm coming for you, Max!" The chase was on! Within seconds, he dived down the stairs, grabbed Rufus' tail and retrieved a drenched Max into his arms. The friends were reunited.

Lewis Hopkins (11)
Waunarlwydd Primary School, Waunarlwydd

The Adventure Awaits!

As Tom dropped them onto the floor, all of the toys awoke. Tom arrived upstairs with a new toy, Raptosaurus. Raptosaurus acted suspiciously. Phoenix greeted him. They all got to know each other. The garage sale was today and one of the toys had been chucked out accidentally. Phoenix went out to save him. Phoenix got taken by a human. The toys spotted the human. Mappy tracked him and all the toys followed. Going through the vent, they saw Phoenix. Eventually, they got Phoenix out of there. Making their way home, they arrived and quickly got back into their positions.

Iyamah Nandra (10)
Waunarlwydd Primary School, Waunarlwydd

The Penguin And The Rabbit

Once upon a time, lived a toy in a bedroom called Percy Penguin. He had a friend called Roger Rabbit. "Hello," said Roger.
"Let's go on an adventure!" exclaimed Percy. So they set off, across the floorboards, being careful not to make a noise. They got through the bedroom and got to the stairs. Roger bounced happily all the way down. Percy, on the other hand, took a little longer because he was a bit fat! At that very moment, Percy fell and bumped into Roger and they fell down the stairs! Suddenly, there was a creak from upstairs...

Natasha Cooper (10)
Waunarlwydd Primary School, Waunarlwydd

Rosie The No-Tail Pony That Sat On A Shelf

One day, Rosie gazed down at the popular toys from the wooden shelf. They were scattered on the floor like a busy city of imagination. Rosie felt alone. She dreamed of being beautiful and new again. Rosie had lost her tail by being played with too much a long time ago. As Rosie saw all the toys playing, she wondered if she could make new friends. On the shelf, she found a fairy and made a wish! "I want to be beautiful," she said.
"No need, you're already beautiful," said the fairy, "your owner loves you for who you are!"

Jazmin Rees (9)
Waunarlwydd Primary School, Waunarlwydd

The Toy That Came To Life

I was playing with my toys before I went for food. Then when I came back, the most amazing thing had happened. Keep reading to find out more. It was the toys, they had come to life. I could hear them talking and moving. I called their names. They replied, "Yes."

"How are you alive?" It was quiet for a moment, then my favourite replied.

"We don't know."

The next day, I told them, "Come on, let's have some fun." We climbed trees and raced around. I could officially call it the best day of my life.

Saffron Ava Williams (9)

Waunarlwydd Primary School, Waunarlwydd

Dr Stipusteine And His Cool Companions

Once upon a time, there was an evil scientist who went by the name of Dr Stipusteine. He would turn green army men into globs of slime for his own army. But then one day, his batteries ran out and everyone started to laugh at him. Dr Stipusteine was very upset and couldn't move. Suddenly, a little blue wind-up toy mouse came along with Duracell long-lasting batteries and put them in Dr Stipusteine. That made him think about how mean he had been and he invited everyone over for dinner. He also stopped turning people into big globs of slime.

Jaydan Paul Davies (11)
Waunarlwydd Primary School, Waunarlwydd

The War Of The Tiny Soldiers In The Castle

As we scanned the castle we raced in through the window. *Whoosh! Bang!* The door burst open as me and my crew hid under the bed. The people were confused as they left the room. We got back up and looted the bedroom. It was pretty blank. We opened the door and went to another room. We looted it too. There was a broom, but nothing good to find until we found some cameras. It wasn't bad, but we'd been hoping for money. Our hopes looked too high to come true. But then... we saw gold!
"Yay! We found money!"

Ryan Aubrey-Cooze (10)

Waunarlwydd Primary School, Waunarlwydd

The Zora Gang

Billy was excited, his friend Sam was over for tea. They were playing with Bailey the dog and Captain Zora, Billy's favourite toy. Sam broke Captain Zora. Billy was sad. Billy took the toy to Dad to fix with his glue, but that didn't work. He took the toy to Mum who had magic plasters that had fixed Billy's leg before, but plasters couldn't fix Captain Zora. Nan came along. She picked up the toy and opened a box. Billy watched. She pulled out a needle and thread. Then she fixed Captain Zora's cape! Billy was very happy!

Callum Jeffreys (10)
Waunarlwydd Primary School, Waunarlwydd

Jessy's Journey

There was a girl called Molly whose parents gave her a doll, which she named Jessy. Molly loved her, she took her everywhere, even to her friend's house. One of her friends called Nia had a dog called Lucy. Lucy stole Jessy, holding the doll in her mouth, and ran off to the beach. Lucy buried Jessy in the sand. "Where am I?" said Jessy. A passing crab replied. "You are in the sand," said the crab, and helped Jessy. Jessy heard Molly crying for her and suddenly saw her. Molly ran to her and hugged her and was happy.

Seren Kathleen Baker (9)

Waunarlwydd Primary School, Waunarlwydd

Finding Home

As it got closer to the closing day of Teddies 'R' Us, everyone was coming to grab last minute bargains. There weren't any toys to be seen except for three lonely toy dogs. The dogs were sad because they were the only toys left, so they decided to escape through an open window. Outside, a friendly-looking boy stopped by them. He smiled, scooped them up and put them in his bag. When the boy got home, he put the dogs on his bed and they were so happy. They sang, "Happy, happy, happy, we've got a new home now!"

Nicole Ashlyn Mort (11)

Waunarlwydd Primary School, Waunarlwydd

Lily And Spidey Spider

In an ordinary house on an ordinary street, lived a little girl called Lily who loved drawing. She drew all the time! On a pleasant Saturday morning, Lily drew a picture of a toy she really wanted! The eyes, the nose and then the mouth. It was called Spidey Spider. "It's lunchtime!" shouted Lily's mum. So Lily rushed over and ate her lunch. Something amazing happened when Lily went for lunch... her drawing came to life! Lily had finally got her Spidey! She was so happy and Lily and Spidey were best friends forever!

Grace Cope (11)

Waunarlwydd Primary School, Waunarlwydd

Raft

I can see the shark getting closer to my raft. I start to panic. What am I going to do? I paddle as fast as I can to get away from the angry shark, but I have to be careful not to let my supplies go overboard. I'm miles from land, I won't survive without my food and water. The shark is getting closer and it has now been joined by a friend. They are circling my raft. This is it!

"Billy, dinner's ready."

"Okay Mum, I'm coming." So I put my controller down and turn my computer game off.

Billy Matthews (10)
Waunarlwydd Primary School, Waunarlwydd

A Mystery In Gondor

Bob was an orphan. His parents had died when he was a baby, so he was moved to an orphanage with his toys Jimmy, Bobby and Harry. When he was eleven, he found a wardrobe that lead to Gondor, a magical land. He and his toys ventured into Gondor only to find a town. As the toys came out of the wardrobe, they started to grow to normal size. They walked over to the town and found them building a school. "Can we help?" Jimmy asked.

"Yes," a worker answered. So in three days they had finished the school.

Evan Williams (11)

Waunarlwydd Primary School, Waunarlwydd

Jeffy Loses His Pencil!

When Jeffy woke up, he realised his pencil was gone! "Where's my pencil?" he cried. Jeffy carried on with his day without his pencil, but nobody found it. Jeffy looked outside and to his amazement, he saw a big castle. Jeffy hurried towards it. In the castle, there were army soldiers everywhere and Lego was scattered on the floor. Jeffy thought, *hmm, this must be where my pencil is.* He walked along the hall and there was the pencil in all its glory. Jeffy returned back home and put the pencil back.

Josh Stockton (11)
Waunarlwydd Primary School, Waunarlwydd

The Doll Who Knows All

An ancient tale tells of the doll that wanders Earth. The doll who knows all. A prepossessing doll who has determined every answer, all meaning, all outcomes and all that was ever sought. And here I am - a leaf, lost astray in the sky. Day after day I scour. I scour with little optimism, acknowledging that myths don't exist. The legend is all that remains, the last dim star gleaming in the twilight sky. One day, the gale ceases to blow, but a hand catches me. The hand of a doll. I found no end to her fathomless gaze.

Sophie Samamh (11)
Waunarlwydd Primary School, Waunarlwydd

One Weird Day With Mr Blobby

One morning, Mr Blobby was in the yard with his friend Mr Potato Head. They ran around the yard but stopped to catch their breath. In Blobbington, it's always dark. Mr Blobby and Mr Potato Head fell onto the floor. They looked up and saw a space shuttle flying above them. The space shuttle used a magnet to pull them in. They landed in mid-air - there was no gravity! A black hole pulled them in and they landed on a planet called Techland. As soon as they landed, the planet blew up and sent them back to Blobbington.

Lowri Burns (9)
Waunarlwydd Primary School, Waunarlwydd

Evil Became Good

Once upon a time, there was an evil bear called Dr Evilbear who ruled the world and enslaved all of the citizens, from children to men. The army saw it and told the captain. "We need to do something!" Then the captain made a plan. They planned the next move the bear was going to make - it was to the bed. They boarded off the area and the bear came and said, "Out of my way." But at that moment, the bear was still and said, "Sorry." Then the bear changed his ways and said sorry to everyone.

Charlie Morgan Davies (10)
Waunarlwydd Primary School, Waunarlwydd

Ski Cross With Bluey Bear

One morning Caerwyn, my owner, asked, "Would you like to go on a ski cross run?" I did not know whether I did or didn't want to, but I said, "Yes!" and off we set.

Looking out of the corner of the bag, my eyes caught the steep, sharp, turning bumps that we were going on. Soon we began to move. Scared, I tucked myself back into the corner of the bag. We were going faster and faster. "Sharp left coming up," shouted my owner. I was not liking it at all. I wish I had stayed in bed.

Caerwyn Richards (11)

Waunarlwydd Primary School, Waunarlwydd

Codi's Adventure In Pillow World!

One day, Codi was bored so he built a colossal pillow fort world. Codi climbed inside and he was in a different world. He was no longer on Earth, he was on Pillow World. Everybody was made out of pillows, even Codi turned into one of them. Codi felt very different indeed as the fellow pillows passed by. The sun started to set, everyone was rushing to their homes. Codi stood there in amazement as a great big dragon came stomping on all the pillows. Codi knew he had to do something, so he slayed the great big beast.

Callum Stockton (11)

Waunarlwydd Primary School, Waunarlwydd

The Unicorn And The Dance

Once upon a time, there lived a dancing toy unicorn. She loved to dance, but unfortunately, she couldn't. However, she never gave up. Millie loved to dance on rainbows. She went to her dance class, but she forgot her routine. She was sad because she had to do another routine. She failed and failed. But this time... she did it! She was able to stand on one foot and do the unicorn dance. Suddenly, the dance teacher came and said, "Want to be in the competition?"
"Yes, I'd love to."

Lola Pascoe (10)
Waunarlwydd Primary School, Waunarlwydd

Timmy Ventures Out

The outside world was feared by teddies, it was a place where anything could happen. Only a few would venture out. Some were lost and others came back. Timmy wanted to go but he kept being told the same thing - it's too dangerous, you'll only get yourself hurt. He was annoyed by this, but one day, he saw an opportunity to leave. They were going away for two weeks so he slipped in a bag and off they went. He thought it was amazing. When they got home, he told his friends about what a lovely time he had.

Sophie Walters (11)
Waunarlwydd Primary School, Waunarlwydd

Pokémon Hunt

In the USA, there are loads of Pokémon trainers. There are gyms where you can put your best Pokémon in to fight. But Lugia never got to go into a gym. He dreamed of going into a gym. Every day he would watch them fight. Then one day, a trainer found him and caught him. Lugia was so happy that he had been caught. He made friends with other Pokémon but all of his friends were going into the gym. Then the trainer put Lugia into a gym and he was the happiest he had ever been in his life.

Theo Chapman (11)
Waunarlwydd Primary School, Waunarlwydd

The Toy Protector

"Dream big princess." That was my wake-up call. Keira had just gone to bed. That was a good thing. My job was to keep away the Monster Marshmallow Man. That night, he was on his way to the bedroom. Keira closed her eyes straight away and started to dream. No company, this will be a long night. "Gurgle, gurgle, gurgle." That was him. I had a very special way of scaring him off. I climbed on the bed and started to dance, waving my arms around and kicking my legs. The monster left.

Keira Davies (10)
Waunarlwydd Primary School, Waunarlwydd

Toy Footballers

It was four o'clock in the morning and the whistle
blew for the football match being held at the table
football pitch in Archie's bedroom. Soon after kick-
off, the first goal was scored by Real Madrid
legend Cristiano Ronaldo. It was now one-nil up to
Real Madrid and West Ham were not happy at all.
In the fortieth minute, almost at half-time, Bale
scored a bicycle kick that hit the crossbar and
went straight in the net. Just when the second half
started, Archie heard the fans cheering.

Archie Davies (10)
Waunarlwydd Primary School, Waunarlwydd

Truffles The Dog

Once upon a time, there was a little girl called Abby. She loved her toys, but there was one toy in particular that she loved. It was a robot dog that could woof, bark and lie down too. She even took it on walks all the time. She was allergic to fur so she could never get a real dog, but she loved this one more than anything. Her mother and father weren't keen on the dog but they didn't mind it because it made their daughter happy. It felt like they had a real dog that they all loved.

Molly Rees (10)
Waunarlwydd Primary School, Waunarlwydd

It Was All A Dream

One morning, I woke up in a claw machine. There were space aliens speaking to me. It was very creepy. An immense shadow crept up and put £50 into the claw machine. I realised that he had as many goes as he wanted. I was hoping he wouldn't pick me, but he did. I was shocked because he got me on his last go. We were going to the man's home, but it was all a dream. I was relieved that I had still got the same owner, not the other man who was ugly, fat and horrible.

Liam Price (9)
Waunarlwydd Primary School, Waunarlwydd

PS4 Fun

It was an ordinary day after school. I went on my PlayStation 4. For some reason, something felt wrong. *Kapow!* I could not see anything but white. I could see everything was a cartoon. Ten minutes later, the game started. I was terrified I was heading for Tilted Towers but I went to Loot Lake. I finally landed and opened a chest, I had the best gun ever. Minutes later, there were two men. I built a base and scanned everywhere. I finally killed them. Victory royale.

Cole Cheetham (10)
Waunarlwydd Primary School, Waunarlwydd

The Magic Cat

One day there was a cat called Rose. She walked down a dark lane. A fox jumped out of a bush. She lifted up her paw and a bunch of sparkles appeared. The fox disappeared. She carried on walking and saw a huge shiny light. She walked in and saw a long stick. It was called a beam. A girl went on the beam and did a cartwheel. The girl also did a handstand. The people were clapping. Rose lifted up her paw and everything was gone. She walked home and ate food and went to bed.

Kady Marie Davies (9)
Waunarlwydd Primary School, Waunarlwydd

Mer Life In The Future

Hi! I'm Noe and this is my story. It was an ordinary day for me until one day my dream came true! I wanted to go swimming so I did, and I soon found out that I had a tail! I found myself in a swamp. I found a boy. A merman! I saw he had a tail. He saw me so I swam away, but he found out that I was a mermaid too. We faced great danger together. We always had each other's backs. Then one day we were turned into figures, but the end's only the beginning...

Mia Cheetham (10)
Waunarlwydd Primary School, Waunarlwydd

Roboman

Once upon a time in a small land of toys, there was a toy called Rainbowman. He loved to dance, he was a champion. He had never been beaten before. But one day, he got beaten by Rainbowdude, his brother. So he challenged him to a dance-off. Who would win, Rainbowman or Rainbowdude? Rainbowman glanced at Rainbowdude and they started. Rainbowman could win if he did his special move. It is almost impossible. He was about to do it. He did it.

Harley Sinclair (9)
Waunarlwydd Primary School, Waunarlwydd

Untitled

Once upon a time, there was a little toy whose name was Bob. He was stuck in the house because he lived with Nana. There were no games anywhere. He couldn't walk much as he had to try not to get caught because he is only a toy and the grandchildren were there. They were always playing with him, but he would cry if they threw him on the floor. He didn't have any brothers or sisters so he was really, really bored.

Jac Hawkins (11)
Waunarlwydd Primary School, Waunarlwydd

Torchy, The Lovey Toy Dragon

It was a normal day and Torchy was being played with by her owner Jemma. The next day, Jemma was getting up to play with her toy, but the toy would not turn on. Then her mother said it needed batteries. A few months later, Jemma got batteries and fixed Torchy and was so so happy. Then she played and played for hours.

Mia-Anne Tabone (10)
Waunarlwydd Primary School, Waunarlwydd

Zong

Jamie was a twelve-year-old who loved writing and illustrating books. While flicking through the pages one day his drawing of a creature named Zong from Planet Saturn appeared in the room next to Jamie in his house. Zong had never seen a house before so he started rummaging through all the cupboards and fridge. He pulled all the food from the fridge and threw them all over the floor. Jamie's house was a mess and his mum was due home. Jamie rushed, opened his book and erased the drawing of Zong, and suddenly Zong was gone for good.

Aron Copeland (10)
Ysgol Yr Eirl, Trefor